# The PHANTOM OF CREEPY HOLLOW

A Mummy Dearest Creepy Hollow
WhoooooooooDunnit?

BY ROBERT KRAUS

WARNER
JUVENILE
BOOKS
A Time Warner Company
New York

Warner Juvenile Books Edition
Copyright © 1988 by Robert Kraus
All rights reserved.

Warner Books, Inc., 666 Fifth Avenue, New York, NY 10103

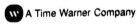 A Time Warner Company

Printed in the United States of America
First Warner Juvenile Books Printing: October 1988
10   9   8   7   6   5   4   3   2

**Library of Congress Cataloging-in-Publication Data**

Kraus, Robert
  The phantom of Creepy Hollow.

  "A Mummy dearest Creepy Hollow whoooooooodunnit?"
  Summary: Mummy succeeds in cornering the Phantom of
the Opry and revealing his secret identity.
  [1. Monsters—Fiction. 2. Humorous stories]
I. Title.
PZ7.K868Pc   1988        [E]        87-40698
ISBN 1-55782-060-0

It is opening night and all the Creeps are going to the Opry.

I SMELL TROUBLE.
HOW ABOUT A BITE AFTER THE SHOW, BABY?
OPRY HOUSE
KEEP YOUR FANGS TO YOURSELF.
TONITE
WEIRDO'S MONSTER BASH
LIP-SMACKIN' GOOD!

The Phantom of the Opry has put bubble bath
in the brass section!

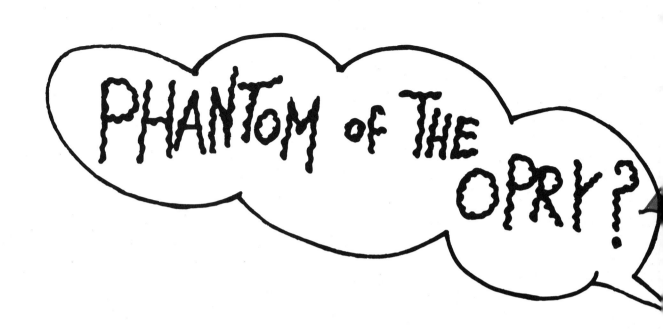

The Phantom presses a secret button and...

Mummy and Noah fall into the
open jaws of hungry alligators.

Is this the end of Mummy Dearest?

Is this the end of Noah Count?

Is this the end of the story?

INCLUDE ME OUT!
JUST WHEN I THOUGHT IT WAS SAFE TO GO BACK IN THE WATER!
I WANT MUM IN MY TUM!
YUMMY YUMMY I LOVE MUMMY.

"Don't snap at me!" snaps Mummy.
She takes out her gator aid kit
and tapes up the gators' jaws.

Mummy rides a gator to freedom.

I'LL BURN HIM!
NEVER FEAR, MUMMY'S HERE!
I'LL SMASH HIM!
I'LL LEARN HIM!

Meanwhile, an angry mob pursues the Phantom.

The Phantom hides in a garbage can and eludes the bloodthirsty mob.

Mummy, great detective that she is,
spots the Phantom peeking out of the garbage can.

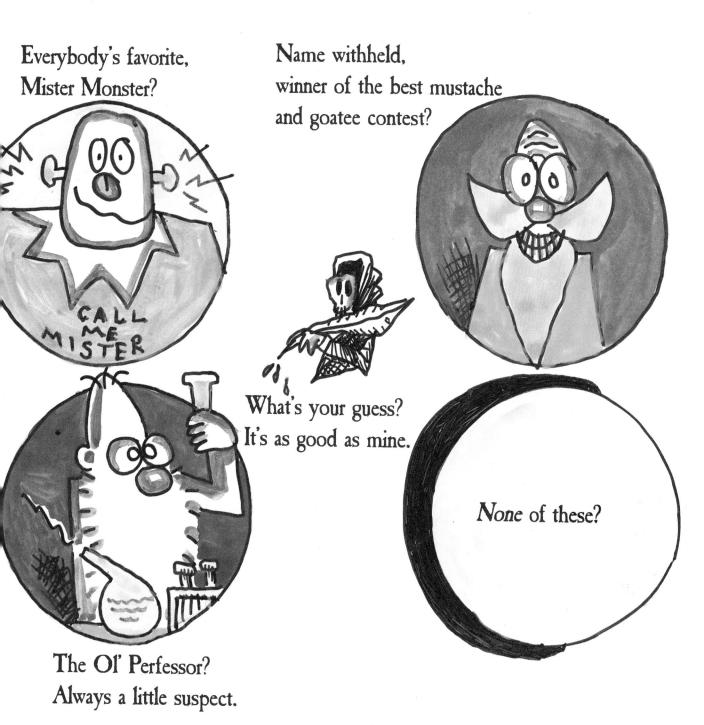

PRACTICE.
I WON'T TURN YOU IN IF YOU PROMISE TO PRACTICE EVERY DAY, BIG GUY.
I PROMISE, I PROMISE. AND THANKS, MUMMY.
WHAT ARE MUMMYS FOR?